S0-AJK-026

Wheeler, Jill C., 1964-
E.B. White /
c2013.
33305228827915
mi   11/20/13

N'S AUTHORS

E.B. WHITE

Jill C. Wheeler

ABDO Publishing Company

visit us at
www.abdopublishing.com

Published by ABDO Publishing Company, PO Box 398166, Minneapolis, Minnesota 55439.
Copyright © 2013 by Abdo Consulting Group, Inc. International copyrights reserved in all
countries. No part of this book may be reproduced in any form without written permission from the
publisher. The Checkerboard Library™ is a trademark and logo of ABDO Publishing Company.

Printed in the United States of America, North Mankato, Minnesota.
102012
012013

 PRINTED ON RECYCLED PAPER

Cover Photo: Corbis
Interior Photos: Alamy p. 19; AP Images pp. 13, 20; Getty Images pp. 5, 12, 15, 21

Courtesy of the Division of Rare and Manuscript Collections, Cornell University Library
pp. 6, 9, 11, 17, 19

Series Coordinator: Megan M. Gunderson
Editors: Tamara L. Britton, Stephanie Hedlund
Art Direction: Neil Klinepier

Cataloging-in-Publication Data

Wheeler, Jill C., 1964-
 E.B. White / Jill C. Wheeler.
  p. cm. -- (Children's authors)
Includes bibliographical references and index.
ISBN 978-1-61783-579-7
1. White, E.B (Elwyn Brooks), 1899-1985--Juvenile literature. 2. Authors, American--20th
century--Biography--Juvenile literature. 3. Children's stories--Authorship--Juvenile literature. I.
Title.
813/.6-dc23
[B]
                                                    2012946387

CONTENTS

NATURAL WRITER

E.B. White had a successful writing career long before he wrote beloved children's books. In fact, many people think of White as one of the best essay writers.

Yet White's name is familiar to most because of his children's books. He wrote the classics *Charlotte's Web*, *Stuart Little*, and *The Trumpet of the Swan*. Each book features memorable human and animal characters.

White often wrote about the delights of New York City. But he also found happiness on his farm in Maine. White was always more comfortable around animals than he was around people.

White won many awards during his career. These include a **Newbery Honor** in 1953 for *Charlotte's Web*. In 1963, he was awarded the **Presidential Medal of Freedom**. He won the **Laura Ingalls Wilder Award** in 1970 and a **Pulitzer Prize** in 1978. All of these awards honored his successful life as a writer.

White was shy and didn't like speaking in front of crowds.

Happy Home Life

Elwyn Brooks White was born on July 11, 1899, in Mount Vernon, New York. His mother was Jessie Hart White, daughter of painter William Hart. His father was Samuel White. Samuel was general manager and vice president of the piano manufacturing firm Horace Waters & Company.

En loved spending time in the family's stable. He cared for birds, dogs, horses, and rabbits.

Elwyn's family called him En. En was the youngest of six children. His oldest sisters, Marion and Clara, were already teenagers when he was born. His brother Albert was 11 and his brother Stanley was 8. His sister Lillian was 5.

En's childhood bustled with activity and music. Samuel brought home instruments for the White children to play. What En's family lacked in talent they made up for with enthusiasm! The Whites also liked to take the trolley to nearby New York City. They visited the zoo and the circus and saw Broadway shows.

Gradually, En's brothers and sisters grew up and left home. With no one to play with, En had to learn how to entertain himself. He was happiest when he was alone with the animals in the family's barn. He spent hours enjoying the sounds, sights, and smells of the stable.

School Challenges

En loved spending his days at home and in the local woods. However, his family insisted that he go to school. This thought frightened him! He begged and pleaded not to go, but he lost the battle. En joined his kindergarten classmates at Lincoln School, P.S. 2.

En always enjoyed learning. Yet he never enjoyed school. He was afraid of crowds and worried that he would be bullied. He most feared being called upon to speak during school assemblies.

The best part of En's school day was recess. He loved standing outside under a big oak tree. When the school day ended, En could go outside again. Partway home he would find his best friend, Mac the collie, waiting to walk with him.

When En was still in kindergarten, his brother Stanley taught him to read. Stanley shared copies of the *New York*

The White family home in Mount Vernon, New York

Times with his younger brother. He pointed to the words and taught En how to sound them out. By the time En reached first grade, he was an excellent reader.

BADGES FROM ST. NICHOLAS

Each summer brought En an escape from school. It also brought him allergies. The family coped by spending part of their summers in Maine. En loved Maine and began writing about the beauty of his summer home. He began a diary around age eight. He kept up the habit for many years.

En also borrowed Stanley's typewriter to put his thoughts on paper. He loved the feel and sound of the big machine as he hammered on its keys. Before he was even 10 years old, En wrote a poem about a mouse. He sent the poem to *Woman's Home Companion* magazine. To his surprise, the magazine published the poem and even gave him a prize for it!

En was inspired. He began writing and sending material to other magazines. One of his favorites was *St. Nicholas*. He was thrilled to see one of his stories printed in its pages in June 1911. The story was called "A Winter Walk," and it won a Silver Badge. En kept sending in stories and drawings. Two years later, he won a Gold Badge for a story about a dog.

In fall 1913, En **enrolled** at

En (center) with his mother, brothers, and sisters in Maine. Lillian is on the right. In the back row are Clara, Stanley, and Albert.

Mount Vernon High School. There, he continued to improve his writing. He became assistant editor of the school's **literary** magazine, the *Oracle*. For this, he wrote about politics and social issues. He also began reading and enjoying the work of other newspaper columnists.

CALL ME ANDY

White graduated from high school in January 1917. In April, the United States entered **World War I**. White did not weigh enough to **enlist** and help the war effort. So, he entered Cornell University in Ithaca, New York, that fall.

Cornell had been cofounded by a man named Andrew White. As a result, the college had a tradition for freshmen with the last name White. They were nicknamed "Andy." White was no exception! In fact, he preferred Andy to Elwyn or En. He began using the name outside of his immediate family. And, he kept using it for the rest of his life.

At Cornell, White was active in the Phi Gamma Delta **fraternity** and sang in a choir. As part of the

A statue at Cornell University honors founder Andrew White.

Manuscript Club, he shared his writing with teachers and fellow students.

White also found success writing for the college newspaper. He worked to

Many students and writers also know White for his work on the writing book The Elements of Style. *White worked on the book by author William Strunk in the 1950s. He had first met Strunk when he took an English class from him at Cornell.*

write columns like the ones he so admired. By senior year, he was editor in chief. And for one of his columns, he won a prize from the Convention of Eastern College Newspapers.

White graduated from Cornell in 1921 with a bachelor of arts degree. Then, the University of Minnesota offered him a teaching position. White turned it down. He wanted to become a writer.

Years of Adventure

After graduation, White worked briefly as a reporter. He had jobs with the United Press and the American Legion News Service. Still, he felt restless.

In spring 1922, White and his college friend Howard Cushman headed west on a long road trip. They spent six months crossing the United States in a Ford Model T. They ended up in Seattle, Washington.

In the fall, White took a job at the *Seattle Times*. He worked as a reporter until June 1923. Finally, he and his editor agreed the job was not the best fit for White.

White left the newspaper and headed to Alaska aboard the SS *Buford*. Years later, he wrote about Ford Model Ts and his adventures in two critically acclaimed essays.

White returned to New York in 1923. There, he found work in advertising. But he did not enjoy it. Luckily, White was about to get his big break.

White's first contribution to the New Yorker *was published under his initials, E.B.W.*

In 1925, White began submitting his writing to a brand new magazine called the *New Yorker*. By 1927, he was contributing weekly. He had a little office and made $30 per week.

Defining the New Yorker

Nearly from its beginning, the *New Yorker* attracted the most famous writers of the time. Readers appreciated its intelligent content and humor. White's writing style and sense of humor were a near-perfect match.

White also was having success publishing his poetry. In 1929, his poetry collection *The Lady is Cold* was published.

The same year, White married fellow *New Yorker* editor Katharine Sergeant Angell on November 13. The couple's son Joel, called Joe, was born on December 21, 1930.

Soon, White returned to his childhood love. In 1933, the Whites purchased a small farm in Maine. They then divided their time between Maine and New York. White loved his time

*Katharine began working at the **New Yorker** shortly after it was founded. She encouraged the magazine's founder to hire White.*

on the farm. The big barn reminded him of the family stable in Mount Vernon. The farm also was located near the ocean, so White could spend time on the water.

MOUSING AROUND

In the late 1920s, White had taken a train trip to Virginia. On the way home, he had a dream about a courageous character on a quest. The character dressed like a human, but he looked like a mouse! White decided the dream would make a good story.

White's nieces and nephews were always after him to tell stories. Yet White confessed to being a poor storyteller. He needed to write stories down first. Then, he could read them aloud. Some of the stories he wrote involved his mouse-like character. He named the character Stuart Little.

In 1938, Katharine encouraged her husband to send his Stuart Little story to a publisher. He did, but the **manuscript** was rejected.

White had battled poor health all of his life. Once, he was feeling particularly ill. He began to worry that his family might not have enough money if he died. So, he went back to work on *Stuart Little*. The book began delighting readers in 1945. White hoped it would help young readers who felt different or odd.

White's work on Stuart Little from around 1935

A movie version of Stuart Little was released in 1999.

HELLO, CHARLOTTE

White raised chickens, cows, pigs, and sheep on his farm. Yet he often struggled with the role of farmer. It was hard to take such good care of animals only to kill them later for meat. He began to think about taking on this touchy subject in another book for children.

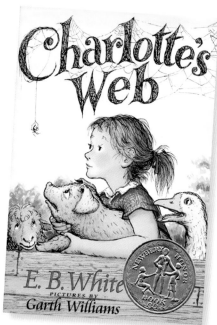

More inspiration for White's story came in 1948. White watched a spider spinning webs in his barn. Then one day, she disappeared. He realized she had spun and filled an egg sac before she went away.

White read books about spiders and talked to spider experts. Slowly, he wrote the story of Charlotte the spider saving Wilbur the pig. *Charlotte's Web* was published in 1952. Since then,

By 2010, Charlotte's Web *had been translated into 35 languages.*

millions of readers have enjoyed this story about death and the power of friendship.

White wrote one more children's book. *The Trumpet of the Swan* was published in 1970. The book is about a trumpeter swan that cannot make noises. He learns to play trumpet and write on a chalkboard.

Katharine White died in 1977. White spent his remaining years on their farm. There he enjoyed writing, canoeing, and caring for his animals. E.B. White died on October 1, 1985, at the age of 86. He left behind writing that both adults and children cherish today.

White felt life just wasn't the same after his wife died.

GLOSSARY

enlist - to join the armed forces voluntarily.

enroll - to register, especially in order to attend a school.

fraternity - a men's student organization, usually having a name made up of Greek letters.

Laura Ingalls Wilder Award - an award given by the American Library Association to an author or illustrator whose works have made a lasting contribution to children's literature.

literary - of or relating to books or literature.

manuscript - a handwritten or typed book or article not yet published.

Newbery Honor - an award given to a runner-up to the Newbery Medal. The Newbery Medal is an annual award given by the American Library Association. It honors the author of the best American children's book published in the previous year.

Presidential Medal of Freedom - the highest civilian honor in the United States. This award is presented to people who have made important contributions to national security, world peace, or cultural efforts.

Pulitzer Prize - one of several annual awards established by journalist Joseph Pulitzer. The awards honor accomplishments in journalism, literature, drama, and music.

World War I - from 1914 to 1918, fought in Europe. Great Britain, France, Russia, the United States, and their allies were on one side. Germany, Austria-Hungary, and their allies were on the other side.

WEB SITES

To learn more about E.B. White, visit ABDO Publishing Company online. Web sites about E.B. White are featured on our Book Links page. These links are routinely monitored and updated to provide the most current information available.

www.abdopublishing.com

INDEX